Boundless Books

Imagination * Collaboration

Copyright 2022

Mark Eischen Creative

Boundless Books

ISBN: 9798842048434

Ruby's Dream Come True

--Story and illustrations by
2022 Summer Session Students
LeMoyne Elementary, Syracuse, NY

Teachers: Clare Kiskadden
Tomoko Stultz

No one really
understood why
Ruby wanted so badly
to fly.

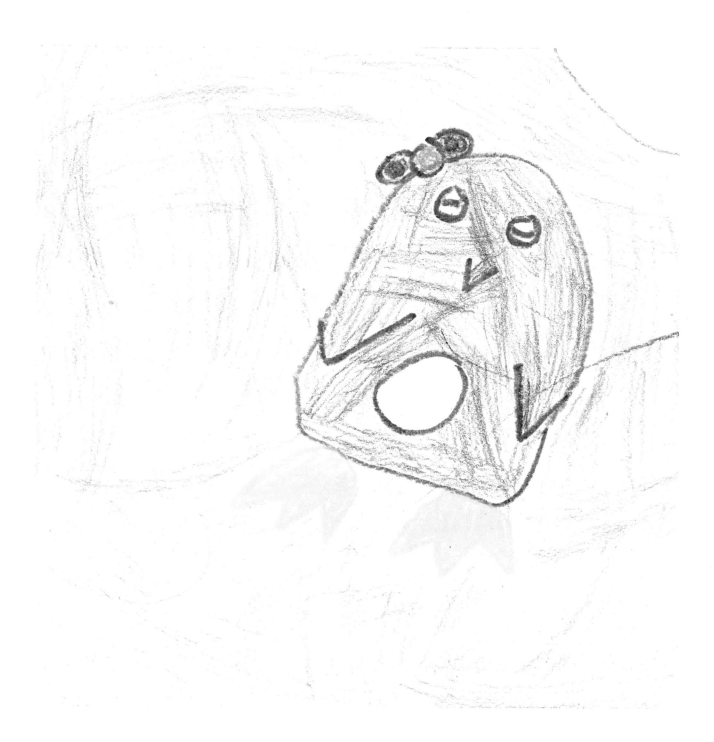

But as silly *to some*,
as it might seem...
day and night,
she held onto her dream.

They all said,
"That dream will never come true.
Just waddle around
like the rest of us do!"

She'd slide on her belly
and close her eyes
and pretend she was way up
high in the skies.

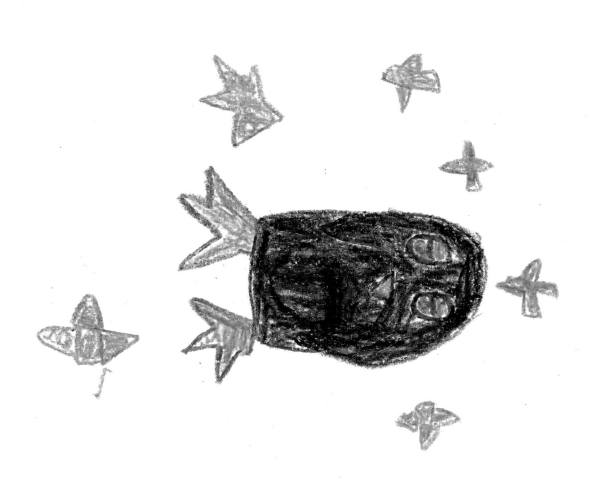

But try as she might,
all year round,
she just couldn't seem
to get off the ground.

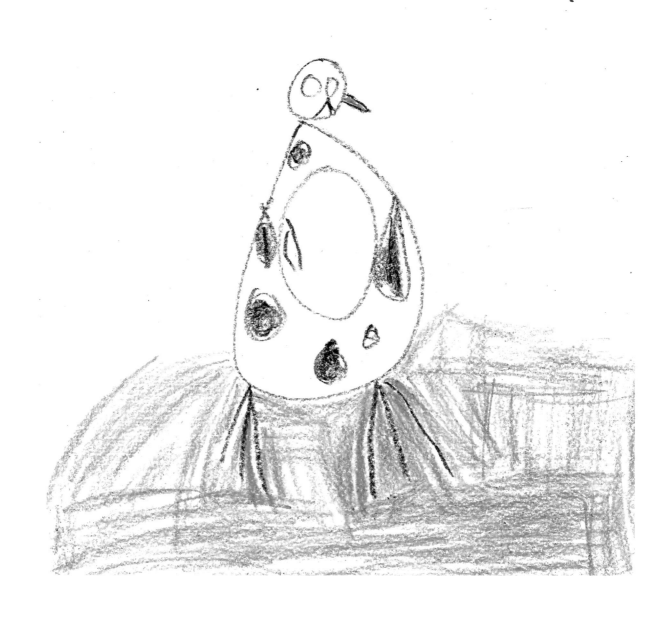

Then one day...
her big idea came!
An idea Ruby knew
would change the game.

She waddled to the top
of the tallest hill.
She looked down the slope,
and felt such a thrill.

The key, she decided,
was to build up some speed.
Ruby knew exactly
what she would need.

She started gathering snow
from all over the place
and piling it up
at the mountain's base.

The other penguins
were all stopping to see...
wondering what
this pile was going to be.

"Is it a giant igloo?"
Someone wondered out loud.
"Or a big waste of time..."
said a voice in the crowd.

Ruby just kept on
working away,
getting closer and closer
to her very big day.

One day she woke up
and knew it was time.
She went to the mountain
and started to climb.

She climbed all the way
to the very top.
She looked down and knew
it was too late to stop.

Ruby took a deep breath
and held her head steady.

What she'd built was a ramp!
And now it was ready.

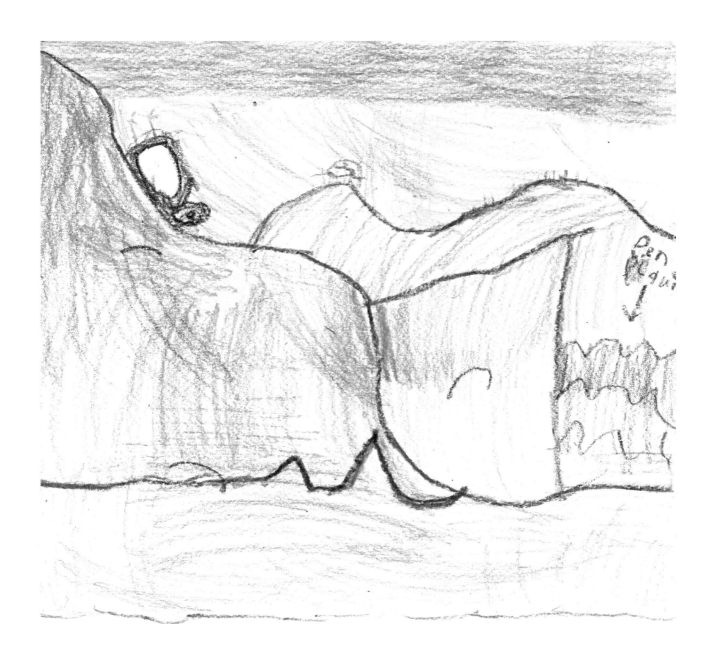

She laid flat on her belly
and gave a little push.
Just a little bit further...
and then...
WHOOOSH!!!!!

No penguin had ever
traveled so fast.
All they saw was a blur
as Ruby went past.

When Ruby hit that ramp,
she was only going faster.
When she finally opened her eyes
She saw clouds flying past her!

Ruby soared through the air
as smooth as could be.
She had never felt
so happy and free.

When Ruby landed
back on the ground
all the penguins
gathered around.

keep line for the ramp

It took lots of hard work
to get to the fun,
but Ruby did what they all said
couldn't be done!

Ruby knew she could make
her dream come true.
If she only believed...
    and the same goes for you!

Author / Illustrators

A'Zarianna Brown
Avery Czyz
Layla Farr
Armond Hobdy
Madison Jimenez
Amelia Johnson
December Jones
Ra' Maj Rucker
Jackson Swann
Lysandro Tejeda
Jasai Williams
Ja'Onna Williams
Maya Withers
Yazan Zain ????
Elijah Barfield
Kensley Brown
Ah'Mahre Butler
Noah Cameron
Kaiden Chrisholm
Levyon Jenkins
Blair Jones
A'Nilah Mathis
Juliani Ortiz
Xavier Pringle
Augustus Taylor
Adrian Tortolini

*Some author/illustrators chose not to be photographed. We greatly appreciate their contributions to this book!

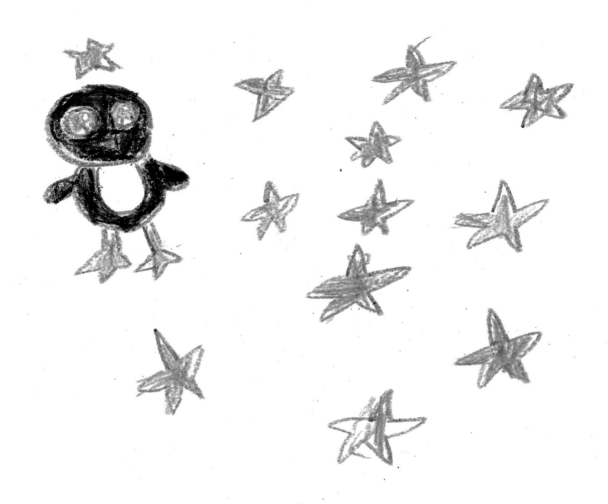

Boundless Books

Imagination * Collaboration

The Boundless Books Program is designed to cultivate creativity and teambuilding in elementary classrooms. Founded in Syracuse, NY by children's book author Mark Eischen, the program consists of classroom visits that take place over a six-week period. During that time, Mr. Eischen guides the students through the writing, illustration and production of their own professionally published children's book... like this one!

www.boundlessbooks.org

Made in the USA
Middletown, DE
28 July 2022

70086596R00029